ROY APPS

DEADLY

The Bloody
Hook

and

Vanishing
Hitchhiker

EDGE
W
FRANKLIN
WATTS

First published in 2012
by Franklin Watts

Text © Roy Apps 2012
Illustrations by Ollie Cuthbertson © Franklin Watts 2012
Cover design by Jonathan Hair
and Peter Scoulding

Franklin Watts
338 Euston Road
London NW1 3BH

Franklin Watts Australia
Level 17/207 Kent Street
Sydney, NSW 2000

A CIP catalogue record for this book
is available from the British Library.

ISBN: 978 1 4451 0337 2

1   3   5   7   9   10   8   6   4   2

Printed in Great Britain

Franklin Watts is a division of Hachette Children's Books,
an Hachette UK company.
www.hachette.co.uk

CONTENTS

The Bloody Hook

Vanishing Hitchhiker

The Bloody Hook

1

This wasn't a part of town he felt comfortable in...

As soon as the movie was over, the audience made for the doors in a rush. Leon took Keisha's hand and led her down through the exit, into the car park.

Leon hadn't really enjoyed the film that much. American romantic comedy wasn't his style; he was more into horror movies, preferably the kind with a lot of blood. But Keisha had chosen the film; it was her birthday, after all. Sixteen today. Leon was determined to make sure tonight would be a night that she would never forget. He had plenty of plans for the rest of the evening. They were going into town to have something to eat, perhaps even sneak into a club…

Keisha really liked Leon. He was fit yes, but he was also thoughtful – and being almost eighteen, he was quite grown-up. Not like most of the boys at school.

Keisha smiled to herself. She liked being sixteen. Earlier that evening, her mum had given her a hug and said to her: "Have a really lovely evening, darling. And now you're sixteen, you don't have to worry about being late. Just as long as you're back by midnight."

Once in the car park, Keisha and Leon made their way to Leon's car. The cinema was on an out-of-town industrial estate, and the traffic was crawling at a snail's pace all the way up to the main road.

"Might as well wait here for a bit," said Keisha, as they got into the car.

Leon frowned. This wasn't a part of town he felt comfortable in, particularly late

at night. The area was controlled by The Warlords, a gang that enjoyed drinking, setting fire to cars and generally looking for trouble. It had been in the local newspaper that The Warlords' leader had just been released from prison. "The Butcher", they called him, because he had a meat hook where his right hand had once been.

As they climbed into the car, Leon turned to Keisha. "I don't know," he said. "Wouldn't it be better to get back into town?"

Keisha said nothing, but instead gave Leon a dazzling smile; a smile Leon couldn't resist. Soon he had his arm around her shoulders and their lips touched…

2

The Butcher

Voices – jeering, yelling; getting closer.
Keisha pulled away from Leon, wiped her
hand on the misted-up window. The car park
was empty, except for a gang of six figures.
They were waving bottles in the air, weaving
their way towards Leon's car.

The Warlords.

One of them walked ahead of the others.
He was larger than the rest. Leon looked
round in time to see the street light catch on
something shiny where his right hand should
be. But it wasn't a bottle. It was a meat hook.

The Butcher.

Keisha screamed as the back window was hit with something heavy. By the time Leon had fired up the engine, The Warlords had surrounded the car, pushing their noses tight against the windows, growling and snarling

like crazed animals. They smashed their bottles against the windscreen, and kicked the doors. As Leon let out the clutch and screeched away, two figures leapt onto the bonnet, grabbing at the windscreen wipers.

Leon frantically spun the car round and they rolled off onto the ground.

The Butcher swung his hook at Keisha's window and the glass exploded. The hook jammed in the door handle. Keisha cried out and grabbed the door's armrest with both hands. She had to stop him getting in! The Butcher leaned in with his hand and tried to grab her arms, but Leon jerked the wheel, throwing him off balance. The chilly night air blasted into the car – The Butcher had pulled the door open! Keisha screamed. Leon glanced round then slammed on the brakes. The door whipped open, pulling The Butcher off his feet. Leon quickly lent over to Keisha's door, and together they forced it closed.

"Put the lock on!" Leon yelled. Keisha snapped down the lock switch.

Leon powered the car forward and glanced up into the rear-view mirror. Leon saw that The Warlords, still shouting and waving their fists, were far behind them now. He accelerated away, putting more distance between his car and the gang.

Then Keisha glanced out of window and saw to her horror that The Butcher was still alongside the car. Keisha screamed again.

"Faster!" she shrieked at Leon. "He's still there!"

Leon swore. Now he could see The Butcher in the side mirror – Keisha was right! He glanced at the speedometer – he was doing close to 40 miles an hour! How could the guy run that fast?

With a squeal of tyres, Leon swung the car violently first left, then right, then left again. There was one last piercing howl from The Butcher, and then he tumbled to the ground.

Keisha sobbed, holding her head in her hands. Leon revved the engine up through the gears. "It's OK," he murmured, turning to Keisha. "He can't get us now."

But Keisha wasn't so sure. Even when she closed her eyes she could still see The Butcher: his twisted smirk, the spittle drooling from his lips, the look in his eyes – and above all, the hook. "Take me home, Leon," she whispered with a shiver. She had no intention of staying out until midnight now. She wanted to be somewhere safe; at home with her mum, watching the TV.

Keisha's feeling of dread began to grow...

It was then that she became aware of a sound above the roar of the car's engine: a rhythmic, metallic knocking coming from her door.

"Slow down, Leon!"

"What? Are you kidding?" But Leon slowed down, just a little. The sound of knocking slowed, and it was fainter, too.

"Can you hear that knocking sound?"

"What?" Leon changed down to third gear. He shrugged. "Something rattling around in the glove compartment, that's all."

Leon put his foot down again. The

knocking became louder again; steady, insistent. It stayed there all the way until they reached Keisha's house, and then it stopped completely. Leon turned off the engine. In the sudden silence, Keisha's feeling of dread began to grow. She started to shake.

Leon leant over towards her. "Keisha, it's all right. There's nothing to worry about now. It was awful, I know, but we saw him off, didn't we – The Butcher? He won't bother us again."

"No?" she replied, doubtfully. She stepped uncertainly out of the car and into the fresh night air.

The warm lights of the house beckoned her, invitingly. She turned to shut the car door.

Keisha's agonising scream ripped through the air. She staggered back from the car, sobbing uncontrollably and sucking in air through her mouth. "No! No!" she cried, shaking her head from side to side. Leon jumped out of the car and raced round to join her. He saw that she was staring at the car door.

Hanging from the car door handle was a meat hook. It had been torn out. Flesh hung from one end, blood was smeared down the side of the door.

That's what had been making the knocking sound.

And in that dreadful moment, Keisha and Leon both knew that The Butcher would come knocking again.

Not just for his bloody hook.

But for them, too.

THE END...

Vanishing Hitchhiker

✝

1

The late evening sky was growing dark...

It was Saturday night. The town centre was hot – packed out with people. Most of them were in noisy groups. As Jake waited to cross the street he watched a quiet couple – hand in hand – walk down the steps into PJ's nightclub. He wished he had a girlfriend he could take to PJ's. Although he was seventeen and had a decent car – a bright red Peugeot – he'd never had a girlfriend.

The fact was, Jake didn't find girls very easy to talk to. The words made sense in his head, but when he spoke they came out wrong.

Jake walked out across the street. Two girls — no more than thirteen either of them — looked his way, nudged each other and giggled. He knew they were laughing at him.

He mooched back to the side street where he had left his car. The air was thick and stuffy. The late evening sky was growing dark, and as he slipped on his seat belt, the first flash of lightning lit up the sky. By the time he reached the brightly painted warehouses on the edge of town, thunder rumbled through the air and rain hammered down. It was the first storm of summer.

As he began the steep climb up Mulberry Hill, Jake changed down a gear, the engine growling. The heavy rain hit the windscreen in great bubbling waves. The wipers struggled to clear it away.

Then, just ahead of him on the edge of the grass verge, his car headlights picked out something… no, not something, someone. He slowed right down and saw that it was a girl. She must have been caught out by the storm, Jake thought.

He pulled up alongside the girl and opened the nearside window. Spats of rain blew into the car.

"Can I give you a lift?"

The girl nodded quickly, opened the door and slipped in. She was wearing an odd-looking pink skirt and a bright green jacket.

2

Her eyes were clear blue...

As they drove off, Jake turned to look at her. Her hair was flat and smelled damp, and he caught just the hint of a smile on her face.

"Are you on your way home?" he asked.

The girl nodded, although she didn't really seem to hear him. She was wrapping and unwrapping her white silky scarf lightly around her fingers.

"Have you been to PJ's?"

This time the girl shook her head, ever so slightly.

"Me neither," said Jake. He felt the need to somehow fill the silence that was growing up between them. "It's full of posers, that place."

As they began to approach the sharpest bend on Mulberry Hill, the girl gasped faintly. Out of the corner of his eye, Jake saw that she was tense – gripping the side of her seat and the door. Her eyes were filled with dread.

"Hey, it's all right," he said. "I know this road like the back of my hand." But even

taking the bend at a steady thirty-five miles an hour, Jake still struggled with the wheel. It was as though the road was trying to throw him off. The camber pulled the car menacingly close to the wet, slippery grass verge – and the deep ditch beyond it.

Once round the bend the girl seemed to relax. She turned and smiled again. Jake saw a face more soft and tender than any he had seen before. Her eyes were clear blue. He reckoned she was sixteen, perhaps seventeen – certainly no older than he was.

"I'm Jake, by the way…" he managed to say.

"I'm Rosie…" he thought he heard her whisper. "Rosie…"

They were nearing the junction at the top of the hill. "Where do you live? I'll take you all the way home, if you like. I mean, the weather out there is really grim." He was gabbling, he knew.

Rosie pointed to a road sign.

"Boxley?"

She nodded and straightened her skirt.

The inside of his mouth
turned suddenly dry...

The unfamiliar lane leading to the isolated village of Boxley narrowed alarmingly. Boxley was its only destination. There were no other villages beyond.

Overhanging hedgerows now cut out some of the worst weather, but oddly there seemed to be a chill in the air. Jake checked the climate control dial: it was showing twenty-one degrees. He boosted it up to twenty-five.

Rosie sat quietly. Jake could sense that something was troubling her. Well, there'd have to be. Why else would she have been standing halfway up Mulberry Hill, all alone, on a night like this? She'd probably been dumped there by her boyfriend after a fight or something. Jake suddenly felt very protective.

"You'll soon be home now," he said, with a reassuring smile.

Rosie nodded.

They passed a dimly lit pub and a couple of cottages. Jake slowed the car to a crawl.

"Say when…"

Rosie jabbed her finger at the window.

"Here… just here…" she whispered.

He stopped the car. A small, white gate glistened in the middle of a long, high hedge. As Rosie put her hand on the door handle, Jake could see that her eyes were full of tears. She opened the door. His heart thumped madly. If he was going to say something, he'd better do it now.

"Look… I can see you're upset and that…
But if you'd like to meet up sometime…
I mean…"

Rosie looked back and smiled – so sadly
this time. But her lips whispered, "Yes…"

She closed the car door gently and then
turned. Jake watched her open the gate and
disappear through the high hedge. Jake saw
that the rain had almost stopped.

As he turned the car round, Jake noticed
something on the passenger seat; Rosie's
white, silky scarf. Jake smiled to himself. He
turned off the engine and picked up the
scarf. It had a curious smell – sort of musty.
Jake couldn't put a name to it, but it didn't
smell like perfume. It wasn't a plain scarf
either, as he'd first thought, but was patterned
with pretty purple flecks.

He got out of the car. The storm had
blown over and a bright moon set everything

with deep black shadows. Jake pushed
open the white gate and walked through.
The angular shapes on the other side
made him stop, and the inside of his mouth
turned suddenly dry. Whatever he had been
expecting to find – a cottage garden perhaps,
or a neat, front lawn – it wasn't this.

Jake was in a graveyard. Not an ancient graveyard with old weather-beaten slabs, but a modern graveyard with bright white marble headstones. The moon lit them up with an eerie glow. A knot of fear tightened in Jake's stomach.

"So, you've come?"

With a jump, Jake spun round. A woman – white-haired, oldish, her face pale in the moonlight – stood just a metre or so behind him against the hedge. She did not seem the least bit surprised to see him standing there. He wasn't sure what scared him most, the shock he'd had when the woman spoke, or the chilling smile she now gave him.

"I'm looking for Rosie…?" Jake stammered.

The woman started to walk away, then turned and beckoned Jake to follow her. She stopped by a gravestone, white as bone, on top of which a carved angel knelt in prayer.

Minutes seemed to pass before Jake dared to look down at the gold-lettered inscription on the grave:

"Rosie"

In Loving Memory of our darling daughter

Rosalyn Anne Harper

Tragically taken from us 28 May 1986

Aged 17 years

"That evening she decided to hitch a lift home – not such an unusual thing for a girl to do in those days. A lorry driver took her as far as the bypass turn at the bottom of Mulberry Hill. She must've started to walk up the hill… At any rate she was hit by a car, you know, on that very sharp bend halfway up. She'd been dead for hours before the police found her in the ditch." The woman turned and held out her hand.

"Now, you have something there that

rightly belongs to me." She pointed with a narrow finger at the scarf that Jake gripped tightly in his fist. Suddenly, he wanted to be somewhere else – anywhere else.

"But she left it in my car just now…" he stammered.

The woman's chilling smile hardened.

"Of course she did, dear. Every year on the anniversary of her death, she hitches a lift and leaves her scarf on the passenger seat. The driver always brings it back, though."

Too late, it all began to connect for Jake: Rosie's old-fashioned skirt, her terror as they'd taken the sharp bend, her faraway look, the strange chill in the car, the musty scent of the scarf...

Jake became aware that the woman was still talking. "You see, the police never found out who did it."

Something else clicked for Jake: "You're Rosie's mum...?"

The woman nodded. "Yes, dear. And a mother will do anything she can for her child. Anything..."

With one sudden movement, she snatched the scarf from Jake. In a flash he saw that the purple flecks on the scarf were really

spots of dried red blood. Desperate to escape, he stumbled backwards, slipped on the wet grass and fell against Rosie's gravestone. Jake struck his head, splattering blood onto the cold, white stone. The dead girl's mother – holding each end of the white scarf tight in front of her – advanced steadily towards him.

THE END...

DEADLY TALES

One book.
Two nightmares.

978 1 4451 0340 2 pb
978 1 4451 0855 1 eBook

978 1 4451 0336 5 pb
978 1 4451 0851 3 eBook

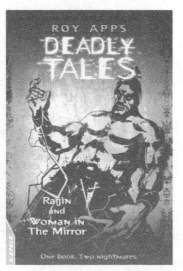

978 1 4451 0341 9 pb
978 1 4451 0856 8 eBook

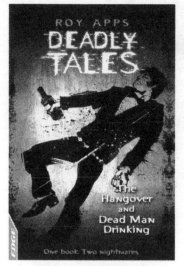
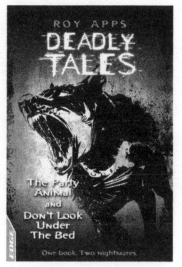

978 1 4451 0339 6 pb
978 1 4451 0854 4 eBook

978 1 4451 0338 9 pb
978 1 4451 0851 3 eBook

Find out more about these books and
others published by EDGE at:
www.franklinwatts.co.uk

Plus visit Roy's website for the latest
news on all his books:
www.royapps.co.uk

DEADLY TALES
TEASER

Can't wait to find out what happens in the other DEADLY TALES urban legends? Well, here's a teaser from The Babysitter:

"Hello?"

Silence.

"Hello?"

Silence. A faint click, then nothing.

Erin sighed, hung up and went back to the sofa. Probably some insurance company, she thought. They were always getting calls from them at home. She had just sat down when the Baxters' phone rang again. This time Erin hit the mute button on the TV remote, cutting off the babble of excited young American voices.

She walked over and snatched up the handset.

"Hello?"

Silence.

"Is that you, Ashley?"

Silence. And then the sound of breathing; at first faint, then becoming steady, heavy. Erin couldn't keep the panic from her voice:

"What do you want?" she said loudly.

Silence. Then a man's voice said, "Sing me a lullaby, Erin..."

✝

Dare you to read the rest in:
DEADLY TALES
Don't Look Behind You
and
The Babysitter